For Martin, your love and support has helped me to create these two fellows. Thanks to my family and you, the reader. Thanks to my best friend, Mr. Hippo, who always cheers me up. -FK

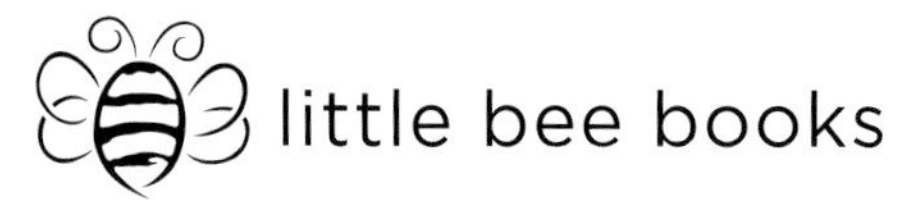

An imprint of Bonnier Publishing USA
251 Park Avenue South, New York, NY 10010

Manufactured in China

First published in Great Britain in 2019 by Boxer Books Limited.
First U.S. Edition
10 9 8 7 6 5 4 3 2 1

Library of Congress Cataloging-in-Publication Data is available upon request.
ISBN 978-1-4998-0742-4
littlebeebooks.com
bonnierpublishingusa.com

The Perfect Sofa

Fifi Kuo

"I think we need
a new sofa,"
said Panda.
"This one is too old."

"Hmmmm,"
said Penguin.
"Let's go shopping!"

"This store has lots of different sofas, Penguin," said Panda.

"Let's try sitting on some," said Penguin.

Too small.

TOO
BIG!

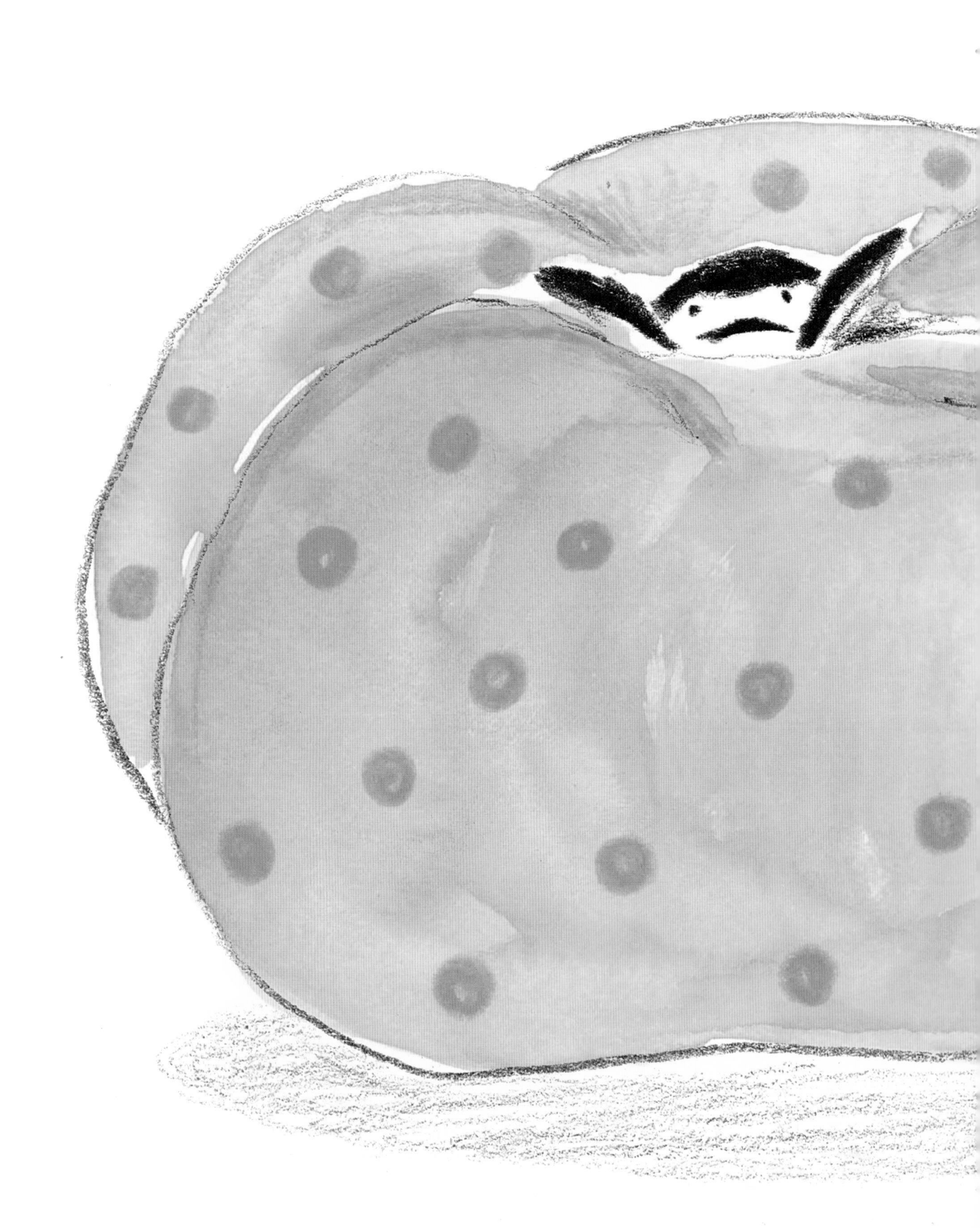

Too squishy.

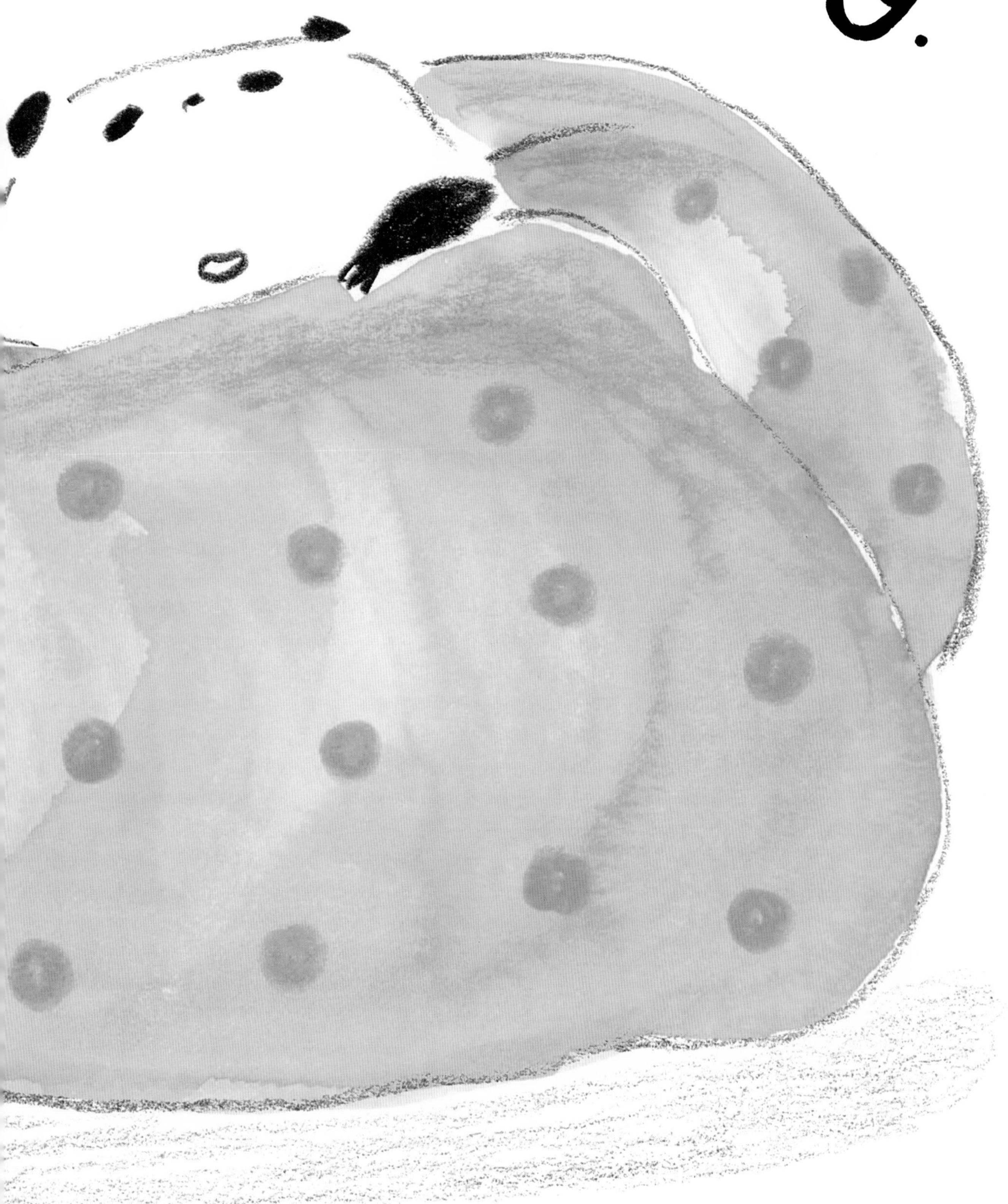

Too colorful!

Too old-fashioned.

TOO MODERN!

Too

e x p e n

s i v e !

"We can't find a

sofa!"

"What a long day,"
said Panda.

"Yes," said Penguin,
"but we did find
the perfect sofa,
didn't we?"